the Wish

Maverick
Early Readers

'King Carl and the Wish'
An original concept by Clare Helen Welsh
© Clare Helen Welsh

Illustrated by Marina Pessarrodona

Published by MAVERICK ARTS PUBLISHING LTD
Studio 3A, City Business Centre, 6 Brighton Road,
Horsham, West Sussex, RH13 5BB
© Maverick Arts Publishing Limited August 2018
+44 (0)1403 256941

A CIP catalogue record for this book is available at the British Library.

ISBN 978-1-84886-371-2

www.maverickbooks.co.uk

Blue

This book is rated as: Blue Band (Guided Reading)
This story is decodable at Letters and Sounds Phase 4/5.

King Carl and the Wish

by **Clare Helen Welsh**
illustrated by **Marina Pessarrodona**

King Carl is at the fair.

He hurls a hoop and...

...he wins a wish!

You can have
one wish!

"Can I have a train and
a dragon?" says King Carl.

"No, you can just wish for
one thing," says the wizard.

"Can I have a gold star and a car?"

says King Carl.

"No, just one thing," says the wizard.

"This and that?" says King Carl.

But the wizard says, "No!"

"That and this?" says King Carl.

But the wizard says, "No, no, NO!"

"Not 2 things...

...not 3 things...

...or 4 things...

...or 5 things..."

King Carl stops.

He thinks long and hard.

"Can I wish for gold?"

says King Carl.

"Yes, you **can** wish for gold,"

says the wizard. 23

The wizard casts his wish spell.

The spell brings King Carl some gold!

Now King Carl can buy lots and lots of things.

Thank you!

Quiz

1. Where is King Carl?
a) At a fair
b) At a park
c) At a beach

2. What game does King Carl play?
a) Football
b) Singing
c) Hoops

3. How many wishes does King Carl win?
a) Three
b) Two
c) One

4. Why does the wizard get cross?
a) He is too hot
b) King Carl wishes for lots of things
c) King Carl wishes for gold

5. What does King Carl do with the things he buys?
a) He shares them
b) He puts them in a box
c) He keeps them all

Turn over for answers

Book Bands for Guided Reading

The Institute of Education book banding system is a scale of colours that reflects the various levels of reading difficulty. The bands are assigned by taking into account the content, the language style, the layout and phonics.

Maverick Early Readers are a bright, attractive range of books covering the pink to purple bands. All of these books have been book banded for guided reading to the industry standard and edited by a leading educational consultant.

To view the whole Maverick Readers scheme, visit our website at
www.maverickearlyreaders.com

Or scan the QR code above to view our scheme instantly!

Quiz Answers: 1a, 2c, 3c, 4b, 5a

Pink

Red

Yellow

Blue

Green

Orange

Turquoise

Purple

Gold

White